Toots
The Fire Farting Dragon

Happy Tooting!

Joni McCoy

D1223852

Written by Joni McCoy
Illustrated by Justin Dunn

Tinlizzy Publishing
Paperback ISBN: 978-1-953814-61-6
Hardcover ISBN: 978-1-953814-62-3
I Was Made This Way

www.YoungBookworms.com

I WAS MADE THIS WAY

My name is Toots. I'm an adorable, responsible, kind,
and gentle dragon - at least that's what my mom always says.

However, I don't feel that way. The kids in school always
treat me differently. They laugh at me and whisper about me.
They don't include me on the playground at recess.
I have no idea why they don't like me, but it hurts my feelings.

Don't we all have differences?
Why don't the other kids want to play with me?

Here I go, off for another day of school.
I'm a dragon, and my tail is a-waggin.
I just know that my positivity and friendliness
will change my classmates' opinions of me today.

We all know that dragons breathe fire. It's a defense
mechanism, but most of all, it's just a cool thing to do.

It all started when I was a baby. I breathe fire like all the
other dragons. Yet, when I'm nervous or excited,
I fart fire too. That's how I got my name:
Toots, the Fire Farting Dragon.

I'm so embarrassed that I can't control my fire farts.

My eyes get glassy, and then I get gassy.

I become nervous and anxious when the kids start teasing me. We all know what happens then:
POW, the fire farting begins!

The kids burst out in laughter, making faces and pinching their noses. My face turns red, and I want to crawl under my desk.

How will I ever control my fire farting?
Does anyone have any ideas?

Upon hearing the recess bell ring, I quickly run out to the playground.

I like to watch the kids play from my safe place, under the shade of a nearby tree. Nobody bothers me here because they are too busy playing.

"Hey guys, do you want to play tag?" I shout.

"I don't think so. We don't feel like getting scorched today," one of my classmates yells back while the kids roll on the ground and laugh.

Daisy is the nicest girl in town. She is always so kind to everyone, including me. She's also the most popular girl at school, and everyone wants to play with her.

She makes me nervous.

On the way home from school, I see her coming and try to hide. Eek! We all know what happens when I get nervous. She spots me: oh no.

"Hey Toots, do you want to go for a walk?"

"Sure!" I respond, climbing out of the tree. What was I thinking? I wonder, no longer concerned about my fire farts.

Am I dreaming?

It's the best day ever! We talk and laugh all afternoon while walking through the country. I don't want the day to end, now knowing what true friendship feels like.

As the day goes on, Daisy and I talk about some things we would like to do together. I can't believe she wants to spend more time with me. Most dragons can't wait to get away from me, but Daisy doesn't even mind my fire farts.

During our walk, I come up with an idea. Tomorrow is Saturday, so I'll have all day to work on my new project.

So very excited, I get up at sunrise before anyone else
in my family.

I'm going to build a hydro pack! It will have a fire hose
and water supply packed into a backpack. From now
on, I'll be well-prepared for accidental scorching and fires.

This is going to change my life!

I spend all day working on my awesome new invention.
The toots start flying, and I'm really not lying.

I'm off to meet Daisy for a day of fun while wearing my hydro backpack so I'm ready for anything.
I see her up ahead, picking flowers, looking very pretty.

I quickly get nervous and feel a doozy coming on: a blast so big that it would endanger anyone around me. I jump into the closest tree to hide.

BAM! A bursting explosion sounds throughout the valley. Daisy snaps her head around and sees me in the tree, engulfed in fire. She runs over to help.

I am so embarrassed until I realize I have my hydro pack.

In one swift motion, I fly out of the tree and snap the switch to "on." Water flows immediately.

Daisy stays right by my side as I douse the flames with water.

"I'm so proud of you, Toots. You're fighting that fire all by yourself," she says, smiling.

I feel such joy: not only because I finally found a true friend but that I can now put out any fires caused by my fire farting. My embarrassment has been replaced with feelings of happiness!

I keep spraying until firefighters arrive on scene. I couldn't save the tree, but with the help of my awesome hydro pack, I prevented the rest of the forest from burning down.

The firefighters offer enthusiastic fist bumps, thanking me for containing the fire.

Some ask if I can make a hydro pack for their crew: what an honor.

The news of the fire spreads through town, and
the fire chief arrives to inspect the damage.

Word spreads about my hydro pack as well, and
the chief asks to check out my backpack.

All the town dragons begin to gather.

I'm used to others whispering about me, but this
is the first time they're saying good things,
cheering "Toots! Toots! Toots!"

My parents, classmates, and Daisy all cheer me on.

Then the fire chief calls me up to the town concert stage. I'm nervous and let out a fire fart, but thankfully, the crowd doesn't mind.

The fire chief officially names me "Toots, the Fire Farting Dragon," the town superhero.

Today, I feel like I've gone from zero to hero!

Daisy immediately recognizes a difference in me:
a confidence that never existed before.

I'll never forget this day or the feeling that comes with
embracing my differences. I was made this way,
and mom is right: it's truly best just to be me.

We all have differences in this world: some of which
you can see and others that are not so visible.

Embrace those differences and display your
uniqueness for all the world to see. After all,
our lives would be so boring if we were all formed
from the same mold!

I walk Daisy home and thank her for her friendship,
letting her know that it has changed my life for the better.
Because of her kindness, I now have so many friends.

Be kind to all, and never make others feel small.

I'm a dragon, and my tail is a-waggin.

Dragons who once teased me are now my friends.

I'm no longer embarrassed by my differences, as
they help make me the dragon I am today.

No matter what, remember that you are enough,
and you always were.